Grub in Love

For Dave with love A.B.

For Lee S. W.

First published in Great Britain in 2010
This edition published 2015
Deepdene Lodge, Deepdene Avenue,
Dorking, Surrey, RH5 4AT, UK
www.bonnierpublishing.com

Text copyright © Abi Burlingham, 2010
Illustrations copyright © Sarah Warburton, 2010

Printed and bound in China

ISBN: 978 1 84812 492 9 (paperback)

1 3 5 7 9 10 8 6 4 2

Grub
in Love

Abi Burlingham
Illustrated by Sarah Warburton

PICCADILLY PRESS • LONDON

This is me,
I'm Ruby.

This is Grub,
he's a grubby, mucky pup!
He's always getting into trouble.
But this time –
you just won't believe it!

Some new people moved in next door.

There was a boy, called Billy.

I was not very happy about that.

I don't like boys.

There was a dog called Tilly too.

Grub was not very happy about that.

Grub crouched by the fence
and growled and wouldn't move an inch.
He shook his head at the flowers.
He shook his head at the fence.
He was definitely not happy.

One day I moved a plank and peeked through the fence.

Billy and Tilly were playing football.

It looked like lots of fun.

I wished I could play.

Grub just growled.

Then, guess what happened?

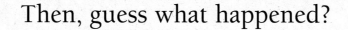

Billy kicked the ball right over **our** fence.

Do you know what Grub did?

He chased it,

he kicked it,

he headed it,

he rolled right over it.

Billy peeked through his side of the fence
and laughed and laughed.
Billy looked like fun.
Perhaps I could like him a little bit,
even though he is a boy.
I wished Grub liked Tilly.
But he just growled.

Then, after the first day
and the second day
and the third day
and the fourth day,
Grub stopped growling.
Do you know why?

He was peeping at Tilly through the fence

and Tilly was peeping at Grub.

Then the trouble really started.

Grub moaned and groaned.

He grunted and grumbled.

He snorted and sniffed.

I said, "Here Grub, dig."

But Grub wouldn't dig.

Do you know what he did?

He hung his head

and his ears went flip flop.

At night he made this crying noise.

Mum covered her ears.

Dad covered his ears.

I covered my ears.

Joe covered his eyes –

I have no idea why.

Mum said, "Grub's in love. He's pining."
It sounded more like whining to me.

Joe's too little to understand.
He thinks Grub has got a cold.

He sat in Grub's basket and patted his head.
"Poor Gub," he said.

In the morning,

Grub wouldn't eat his food.

He just stared at it.

Then he stared at me.

Then I scratched his floppy ears.

That cheered him up a bit!

Billy said Tilly was just the same.
Billy said Tilly would only eat cheese
and crusty bread.
I think Tilly might be French.

We bought Grub a toy bird to cheer him up.

"Look, Grub!" I said.

"You'll love her.

She's got a squeak."

But Grub didn't love her at all,

not one bit.

I think Mum is right. Grub loves Tilly.

The next day, Grub started digging again –
under the fence!
Do you know what Tilly did?
She started digging too!
I pulled and pulled to get Grub back.
Billy pulled and pulled to get Tilly back.
Then they both started whining.
"I've had enough!" said Mum.

So me and Billy had a meeting by the fence.

It was very important.

We talked about Grub and Tilly.

Then we each had a lemonade lolly

and hunted for snails.

I collected them in a bucket.

We had nine!

But we still didn't know what to do about

Grub and Tilly.

That night,
Grub scratched and scratched and scratched
at the back door
and made all the paint come off.
It looked such a mess.
"That's it!" said Mum, "I really have had enough."

So the next day my mum and Billy's mum
and me and Billy
decided to have a picnic,
all of us together,
with Grub and Tilly!

It was the best picnic ever.
We had bread and cheese and
strawberry tarts
and we played football.

Do you know what Grub and Tilly did?

They raced around the trees,

they chased each other's tails

and they ran so far that we had to go and look for them.

When we found them,

Grub had the waggiest tail I have ever seen.

In the morning, Grub ate all his food.

"Good dog, Gub!" said Joe.

Then Grub dug three holes
in the garden.

"Bad dog, Gub!" said Joe.

But it wasn't bad really.

It was good . . .

because a digging Grub
was a happy Grub.

"Would you like to go for a picnic
again with Tilly?" I asked Grub.
Do you know what Grub did?

He gave me the
BIGGEST, muckiest hug
ever!